PRINCESS STORIES

THE STORY OF CINDERELLA
TWELVE DANCING PRINCESSES
THE FROG-PRINCE
SLEEPING BEAUTY

"If you want your children to be intelligent, read them fairy tales.
If you want them to be more intelligent, read them more fairy tales."

– Albert Einstein

To our mother, who wanted us all to be intelligent.

DESIGNED BY
STEPHANIE MEYERS

THE STORY OF CINDERELLA

There once lived a gentleman, who, on becoming a widower, married a most haughty woman for his second wife. The lady had two daughters by a former marriage, equally proud and disagreeable as herself, while the husband had one daughter of the sweetest temper and most angelic disposition.

No sooner was the wedding over, than the stepmother began to show her bad temper. She could not bear her stepdaughter's good qualities, that only showed up her daughters' unfavorable ones still more obviously, and she accordingly compelled the poor girl to do all the drudgery of the household. It was she who washed the dishes, and scrubbed down the stairs, and polished the floors in my lady's chamber, and in those of her two daughters. And while the latter slept on good featherbeds in elegant rooms, furnished with full-length looking-glasses, their stepsister lay in a wretched loft on an old straw mattress. Yet the poor thing bore this ill treatment very meekly and did not dare complain to her father when he returned from his frequent journeys.

When her work was done, she would sit in the chimney corner amongst the cinders, which had caused the nickname of Cinderella to be given her by the family. Yet, for all her shabby clothes, Cinderella was a hundred times prettier than her sisters.

It happened that the king's son gave a ball, to which he invited all the nobility; As our two young ladies made a great figure in the world, they were included in the list of invitations. So they began to be very busy choosing which gown would be the most becoming. Here was fresh work for poor Cinderella, for it was she who was to starch and get up their ruffles, and iron all their fine linen. Nothing but dress was talked about for days together.

"I," said the eldest, "shall put on my red velvet dress with my point-lace trimmings."

"And I," said the younger sister, "shall wear my usual petticoat, but shall set it off with my gold brocaded train and my circlet of diamonds."

They called in Cinderella for her advice, as she had such good taste, and Cinderella not only advised them well, but also offered to dress their hair which they were pleased to accept.

While she was busy with this, the sisters said to her, "Oh, Cinderella, would you like to go to the ball?"

"No, you are teasing me," replied the poor girl. "It is not for such as I to go to balls."

"True enough, they chuckled. "Folks would laugh to see a Cinderella at a court ball."

Anyone other than Cinderella would have made their hair a mess to punish them for their impertinence, but she was so good-natured that she made them both look fabulous.

The long-wished-for evening came at last, and off they set. Cinderella's eyes followed them as long as she could, and then she began to weep. Her godmother now appeared, and seeing her in tears inquired what was the matter.

"I wish … I wish," began the poor girl, but tears choked her utterance.

"You wish that you could go to the ball," interrupted her godmother, who was a fairy.

"Indeed I do!" said Cinderella with a sigh.

"Well, then, if you will be a good girl, you shall go," said her godmother. "Now, fetch me a pumpkin from the garden."

Cinderella flew to gather the finest pumpkin she could find, though she could not understand how it was to help her to go to the ball. But her godmother simply touched it with her wand, and it was immediately changed into a golden coach. She then went to the mousetrap, where she found six live mice, and bidding Cinderella let them out one by one, she changed each mouse into a fine dapple-grey horse by a stroke of her wand. With another stroke of her wand, she turned a fine rat, who happened to have a tremendous pair of whiskers, into a coachman with the finest moustache ever seen.

She then said: "Now go into the garden and bring me six lizards, which you will find behind the watering-pot." These were no sooner brought than they were turned into six footmen who got up behind the coach just as naturally as if they had done nothing else all their lives.

The fairy godmother then said to Cinderella: "Off you go then, you're all set for the ball."

"But must I go in these dirty clothes?" said Cinderella, timidly. Her godmother merely touched her with her wand, and her shabby clothes were changed to a dress of gold and silver tissue, all ornamented with precious stones. For her feet she gave her the prettiest pair of glass slippers ever seen. As Cinderella got into the carriage, her fairy godmother warned her not to stay beyond midnight, as should she remain a moment longer at the ball, her coach would again become a pumpkin, her horses mice, her footmen lizards, while her clothes would return to their former shabby condition. Cinderella promised she would not fail to leave the ball before midnight and set off in delight.

When Cinderella's horse-drawn carriage arrived at the ball, the king's son was informed that some great princess, unknown at court, had just arrived. He went to hand her out of her carriage and brought her into the hall where the company was assembled. The moment she appeared, all conversation was hushed, the violins ceased playing, and the dancing stopped short; so great was the sensation produced by the stranger's beauty. A confused murmur of admiration fluttered through the crowd, and many exclaimed, "How surpassingly lovely she is!" Even the king, old as he was, could not forbear admiring her like the rest, and he whispered to the queen that she was certainly the fairest and comeliest woman he had seen for many a long day. The ladies were all busy examining her head-dress and her clothes, in order to get similar ones the very next day.

After leading her to the place to which her rank seemed to entitle her, the king's son requested her hand for the next dance, and she displayed so much grace as to increase the admiration her beauty had raised in the first instance. An elegant supper was next brought in, but the young prince was so taken up with gazing at the fair stranger, that he did not partake of a morsel.

Throughout the evening, the king's son never left Cinderella's side, and kept paying her the most flattering attentions. The young lady was just as taken with him. So it came to pass that she forgot her godmother's warning, and, indeed, lost track of the time so completely that before she thought it could be eleven o'clock, she was startled at hearing the first stroke of midnight. In the middle of a waltz, she pulled herself out of the prince's arms and flew away like a startled fawn.

The prince attempted to follow her, but she was too swift for him. Only, as she flew, she dropped one of her glass slippers which he picked up very eagerly.

Cinderella reached home quite out of breath, without either coach or footmen, and with only her shabby clothes on her back. Nothing, in short, remained of her recent magnificence, save a little glass slipper – the match to the one she had lost.

On reaching home, she found her godmother and thanked her profusely for the wonderful night. She was still relaying to her godmother all that had happened at court when her two stepsisters knocked at the door. Cinderella went and let them in, pretending to yawn and stretch herself, and rub her eyes, and saying:

"How late you are!" just as if she was woke up out of a nap; though, truth to say, she had never felt less disposed to sleep in her life.

"If you had been to the ball," said one of the sisters, "you would not have thought it late. There came the most beautiful princess ever seen who knew us by name."

Cinderella could scarcely contain her delight and inquired the name of the princess. But they replied that nobody knew her name, and that the king's son was in great trouble about her and would give the world to know who she could be.

They told Cinderella that the beautiful princess had run away as soon as midnight had struck, and so quickly as to drop one of her dainty glass slippers, which the king's son had picked up and was looking at most fondly during the remainder of the ball. Indeed, it seemed beyond a doubt that he was deeply enamored of the beautiful creature to whom it belonged.

They spoke truly enough, for a few days afterwards, the king's son caused a proclamation to be made, by sound of trumpet all over the kingdom to the effect that he would marry her whose foot should be found to fit the slipper exactly. So the slipper was first tried on by all the princesses, then by all the duchesses, and next by all the persons belonging to the court – but in vain. It was then carried to the two sisters, who tried with all their might to force their feet into its delicate proportions, but with no better success.

Cinderella, who was present, and recognized her slipper, now laughed, and said: "Suppose I were to try?" Her stepsisters ridiculed such an idea, but the gentleman who was appointed to try the slipper, having looked attentively at Cinderella and perceived how beautiful she was, said that it was but fair she should do so, as he had orders to try it on every young maiden in the kingdom.

Accordingly, having requested Cinderella to sit down, she no sooner put her little foot to the slipper, than she drew it on, and it fit like a glove. The sisters were quite amazed, but their astonishment increased ten fold when Cinderella drew the fellow slipper out of her pocket and put it on. Her godmother then made her appearance, and having touched Cinderella's clothes with her wand, made them still more magnificent than those she had previously worn. Her two stepsisters now recognized her for the beautiful stranger they had seen at the ball, and falling at her feet, implored her forgiveness for their unworthy treatment and all the insults they had heaped upon her head. Cinderella raised them saying, as she embraced them, that she not only forgave them with all her heart, but wished for their affection. She was then taken to the palace of the young prince, in whose eyes she appeared yet more lovely than before, and who married her shortly after.

Cinderella, who was as good as she was beautiful, allowed her stepsisters to lodge in the palace, and gave them in marriage, that same day, to two lords belonging to the court. And they all lived happily ever after.

TWELVE DANCING PRINCESSES

There was a king who had twelve beautiful daughters. They slept in twelve beds all in one room. When they went to bed, the doors were shut and locked up. But every morning, their shoes were found to be quite worn through as if they had been danced in all night, and yet nobody could find out how it happened or where they had been.

Then the king made it known to all the land, that if any person could discover the secret and find out where it was that the princesses danced in the night, he would have his choice of the princesses and rule the kingdom after the king's death; but whoever tried and did not succeed, after three days and nights, would be banished from his kingdom.

A king's son soon came. He was well entertained, and in the evening was taken to the chamber next to the one where the princesses lay in their twelve beds. There he was to sit and watch where they went to dance, and in order that nothing might pass without his hearing it, the door of his chamber was left open. But the king's son soon fell asleep. When he awoke in the morning, he found that the princesses had all been dancing, for the soles of their shoes were full of holes. The same thing happened the second and third night, so the king ordered him banished. After him, came several others, but they had all the same luck.

Now it chanced that an old soldier, who had been wounded in battle and could fight no longer, passed through the country where this king reigned. And as he was traveling through a wood, he met an old woman who asked him where he was going.

"I hardly know where I am going or what I had better do," said the soldier, "but I think I should like very well to find out where it is that the princesses dance, and then in time, I might be a king."

"Well," said the old dame, "that is no very hard task. Only take care not to drink any of the wine which one of the princesses will bring to you in the evening, and as soon as she leaves you, pretend to be fast asleep." Then she gave him a cloak and said, "As soon as you put that on you will become invisible, and you will then be able to follow the princesses wherever they go." When the soldier heard all this good counsel, he determined to try his luck. So he went to the king, and said he was willing to undertake the task.

He was as well received as the others had been. The king ordered fine royal robes to be given to him, and when the evening came, he was led to the outer chamber. Just as he was going to lie down, the eldest of the princesses brought him a cup of wine, but the soldier threw it all away secretly, taking care not to drink a drop. Then he laid himself down on his bed, and in a little while, began to snore very loudly as if he was fast asleep. When the twelve princesses heard this, they laughed heartily, and the eldest said, "This fellow too might have done a wiser thing than face banishment in this way!" Then they rose up and opened their drawers and boxes, and took out all their fine clothes, and dressed themselves at the mirror, and skipped about as if they were eager to begin dancing. But the youngest said,

"I don't know how it is, while you are so happy I feel very uneasy. I am sure some mischance will befall us."

"You simpleton," said the eldest, "you are always afraid. Have you forgotten how many kings' sons have already watched in vain? And as for this soldier, even if I had not given him his sleeping draught, he would have slept soundly enough."

When they were all ready, they went and looked at the soldier. He snored on and did not stir hand or foot, so they thought they were quite safe. The eldest went up to her own bed and clapped her hands. The bed sank into the floor, and a trap-door flew open. The soldier saw them going down through the trap-door one after another, the eldest leading the way. Thinking he had no time to lose, he jumped up, put on the cloak which the old woman had given him, and followed them. But in the middle of the stairs, he trod on the gown of the youngest princess, and she cried out to her sisters,

"All is not right! Someone took hold of my gown!"

"You silly creature!" said the eldest. "It is nothing but a nail in the wall."

Then down they all went, and at the bottom, they found themselves in a most delightful grove of trees. The leaves were all of silver and glittered and sparkled beautifully. The soldier wished to take away some token of the place, so he broke off a little branch, and there came a loud noise from the tree. Then the youngest daughter said again,

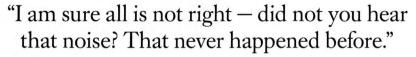

"I am sure all is not right — did not you hear that noise? That never happened before."

But the eldest said, "It is only our princes who are shouting for joy at our approach."

Then they came to another grove of trees where all the leaves were of gold, and afterwards to a third, where the leaves were all glittering diamonds. The soldier broke a branch from each, and every time there was a loud noise which made the youngest sister tremble with fear. But the eldest still said it was only the princes, who were crying for joy. So they went on till they came to a great lake. At the side of the lake, there lay twelve little boats with twelve handsome princes in them, who seemed to be waiting there for the princesses.

One of the princesses went into each boat, and the soldier stepped into the same boat with the youngest. As they were rowing over the lake, the prince who was in the boat with the youngest princess and the soldier said, "I do not know why it is, but though I am rowing with all my might, we do not get on so fast as usual, and I am quite tired. The boat seems very heavy today."

"It is only the heat of the weather," said the princess. "I feel it very warm, too."

On the other side of the lake stood a fine illuminated castle, from which came the merry music of horns and trumpets. There they all landed and went into the castle where each prince danced with his princess. The soldier, who was all the time invisible, danced with them, too. And when any of the princesses had a cup of wine set by her, he drank it all up, so that when she put the cup to her mouth it was empty. At this, too, the youngest sister was terribly frightened, but the eldest always silenced her. They danced on till three o'clock in the morning. By then all their shoes were worn out, so that they were obliged to leave. The princes rowed them back again over the lake (but this time the soldier placed himself in the boat with the eldest princess). On the opposite shore, they took leave of each other – the princesses promising to come again the next night.

When they came to the stairs, the soldier ran on before the princesses and laid himself down. As the twelve sisters slowly came up very much tired, they heard him snoring in his bed, so they said, "Now all is quite safe." They undressed themselves, put away their fine clothes, pulled off their shoes, and went to bed.

In the morning, the soldier said nothing about what had happened. Determined to see more of this strange adventure, he went again the second and third night. And everything happened just as before; the princesses danced each time till their shoes were worn to pieces and then returned home. However, on the third night, the soldier carried away one of the golden cups as a token of where he had been.

As soon as the time came when he was to declare the secret, he was taken before the king with the three branches and the golden cup. The twelve princesses stood listening behind the door to hear what he would say.

And when the king asked him,
"Where do my twelve daughters dance at night?"
he answered,
"With twelve princes in a castle underground."

And then he told the king all that had happened and showed him the three branches and the golden cup which he had brought with him. Then the king called for the princesses and asked them whether what the soldier said was true. When they saw that they were discovered, and that it was of no use to deny what had happened, they confessed it all. And the king asked the soldier which of the princesses he would choose for his wife. He answered, "I am not very young, so I will have the eldest."

And they were married that very day, and the soldier was chosen to inherit the king's throne.

THE FROG-PRINCE

One fine evening, a young princess put on her bonnet and clogs and went out to take a walk by herself in a wood. When she came to a cool spring of water that rose in the midst of it, she sat herself down to rest awhile. Now she had a golden ball in her hand, which was her favorite plaything. and she was always tossing it up into the air and catching it again as it fell. After a time, she threw it up so high that she missed catching it as it fell, and the ball bounded away and rolled along upon the ground, till at last it fell down into the spring. The princess looked into the spring after her ball, but it was very deep – so deep that she could not see the bottom of it. Then she began to bewail her loss and said, "Alas! If I could only get my ball again, I would give all my fine clothes and jewels, and everything that I have in the world."

Whilst she was speaking, a frog put its head out of the water and said,

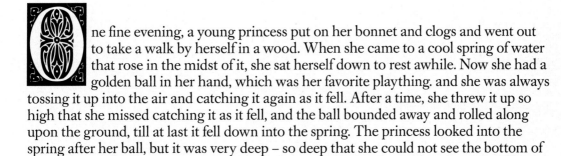

"Princess, why do you weep so bitterly?"

"Alas!" said she. "What can you do for me, you nasty frog? My golden ball has fallen into the spring."

The frog said, "I want not your pearls and jewels and fine clothes, but if you will love me, and let me live with you, and eat from your golden plate, and sleep upon your bed, I will bring you your ball again."

"What nonsense," thought the princess, "this silly frog is talking! He can never even get out of the spring to visit me, though he may be able to get my ball for me. Therefore, I will tell him he shall have what he asks."

So she said to the frog, "Well, if you will bring me my ball, I will do all you ask."

Then the frog put his head down and dived deep under the water. After a little while, he came up again with the ball in his mouth, and threw it on the edge of the spring. As soon as the young princess saw her ball, she ran to pick it up. She was so overjoyed to have it in her hand again, that she never thought of the frog, but ran home with it as fast as she could.

The frog called after her, "Stay, princess, and take me with you as you said." But she did not stop to hear a word.

The next day, just as the princess had sat down to dinner, she heard a strange noise—tap, tap—plash, plash—as if something was coming up the marble staircase. Soon afterwards there was a gentle knock at the door, and a little voice cried out and said:

"Open the door, my
princess dear,
Open the door to
thy true love here!
And mind the words
that thou and I said
By the fountain cool,
in the greenwood
shade."

The princess ran to the door and opened it, and there she saw the frog whom she had quite forgotten. At this sight, she was sadly frightened, and shutting the door as fast as she could, came back to her seat. The king, her father, seeing that something had frightened her, asked her what was the matter.

"There is a nasty frog," said she, "at the door, that lifted my ball for me out of the spring this morning. I told him that he should live with me here, thinking that he could never get out of the spring, but there he is at the door, and he wants to come in."

While she was speaking the frog knocked again at the door, and said:

"Open the door, my princess dear,
Open the door to thy true love here!
And mind the words that thou and I said
By the fountain cool, in the greenwood shade."

Then the king said to the young princess,
"As you have given your word, you must keep it.
So go and let him in."

She did so, and the frog hopped into the room, and then straight on—tap, tap—plash, plash—from the bottom of the room to the top, till he came up close to the table where the princess sat.

"Pray lift me upon chair," said he to the princess, "and let me sit next to you."

As soon as she had done this, the frog said, "Put your plate nearer to me, that I may eat out of it."

This she did, and when he had eaten as much as he could, he said,

"Now I am tired. Carry me upstairs and put me into your bed."

And the princess, though very unwilling, took him up in her hand and put him upon the pillow of her own bed where he slept all night long. As soon as it was light, he jumped up, hopped downstairs, and went out of the house.

"Now, then," thought the princess, "at last he is gone, and I shall be troubled with him no more." But she was mistaken, for when night came again, she heard the same tapping at the door. And the frog came once more and said:

"Open the door, my princess dear,
Open the door to thy true love here!
And mind the words that thou and I said
By the fountain cool, in the greenwood shade."

And when the princess opened the door, the frog came in and slept upon her pillow as before till the morning broke. And the third night he did the same. But when the princess awoke on the following morning, she was astonished to see, instead of the frog, a handsome prince, gazing on her with the most beautiful eyes she had ever seen, and standing at the head of her bed.

He told her that he had been enchanted by
a spiteful fairy, who had changed him into a
frog, and that he had been fated so to abide till
some princess should take him out of the spring
and let him eat from her plate, and sleep upon her
bed for three nights.

"You," said the prince, "have broken his cruel charm, and now I have nothing to wish for but that you should go with me into my father's kingdom, where I will marry you, and love you as long as you live."

The young princess, you may be sure, was not long in saying, "Yes!" As they spoke, a coach drove up with eight beautiful horses decked with plumes of feathers and a golden harness. Behind the coach rode the prince's servant, faithful Heinrich, who had bewailed the misfortunes of his dear master during his enchantment so long and so bitterly, that his heart had well-nigh burst.

They then took leave of the king and got into the
coach with eight horses, and all set out,
full of joy and merriment, for the prince's kingdom,
which they reached safely. And there they lived
happily a great many years.

SLEEPING BEAUTY

Once, there was a royal couple who grieved excessively because they had no children. When at last, after long waiting, the queen presented her husband with a little daughter. His majesty showed his joy by giving a christening feast so grand that the like of it was never seen before. He invited all the fairies in the land — there were seven altogether — to be godmothers to the little princess; hoping that each might bestow on her some good gift, as was the custom of good fairies in those days.

After the ceremony, all the guests returned to the palace where there was set before each fairy-godmother a magnificent covered dish with an embroidered table-napkin, and a knife and fork of pure gold, studded with diamonds and rubies. But alas! As they placed themselves at the table, there entered an old fairy who had not been invited, because she had left the king's dominion on a tour of pleasure and had not been heard of until this day. His majesty, much troubled, had a place set for her, but it was of common everyday dishes, for he had ordered from his jeweler only seven gold dishes for the seven invited fairies. The elderly fairy felt quite neglected and muttered angry menaces, which were overheard by one of the younger fairies who chanced to sit beside her. This good godmother, afraid of harm to the pretty baby, hastened to hide herself behind the tapestry in the hall. She did this because she wished all the others to speak first — so that if any ill gift were bestowed on the child, she might be able to counteract it.

After dinner, six fairies offered their good wishes which, unlike most wishes, were sure to come true. The fortunate little princess was to grow up the fairest woman in the world, to have a temper sweet as an angel, to be perfectly graceful and gracious, to sing like a nightingale, to dance like a leaf on a tree, and to possess every accomplishment under the sun. Then the old fairy's turn came. Shaking her head spitefully, she uttered the wish that when the baby grew up into a young lady and learned to spin, she might prick her finger with the spindle and die of the wound.

At this terrible prophecy, all the guests shuddered, and some of the more tender-hearted began to weep. The lately happy parents were almost out of their wits with grief, upon which the wise young fairy appeared from behind the tapestry, saying cheerfully, "Your majesties may comfort yourselves. The princess shall not die. I have no power to alter the ill fortune just wished her by my ancient sister. Her finger must be pierced, and she shall then sink, not into the sleep of death, but into a sleep that will last a hundred years. After that time is ended, the son of a king will find her, awaken her, and marry her."

Immediately all the fairies vanished.

The king, in the hope of avoiding his daughter's doom, issued an edict forbidding all persons to spin, and even to have spinning-wheels in their houses. But it was in vain. One day, when she was just fifteen years of age, the king and queen left their daughter alone in one of their castles when, wandering about at her will, she came to an ancient tower, climbed to the top of it, and there found a very old woman — so old and deaf that she had never heard of the king's edict — busy with her wheel.

"What are you doing, good woman?" asked the princess.

"I'm spinning, my pretty child."

"Ah, how charming! May I try to spin also?"

She had no sooner taken up the spindle than, being lively and obstinate, she handled it so awkwardly and carelessly that the point pierced her finger. Though it was just a small wound, she fainted away at once and dropped silently down on the floor. The poor frightened old woman called for help. Shortly came the ladies in waiting, who tried every means to restore their young mistress. But all their care was useless. She lay, beautiful as an angel, the color still lingering in her lips and cheeks; her fair bosom

softly stirred with her breath. Only her eyes were fast closed. When the king, her father, and the queen, her mother, saw her, they all had happened as the cruel fairy intended. But they also knew that their daughter would not sleep forever, though after one hundred years it was not likely they would either of them behold her awakening. Until that happy hour should arrive, they determined to leave her in repose. They sent away all the physicians and attendants, and themselves sorrowfully laid her upon a bed of embroidery in the most elegant apartment of the palace. There she slept and looked like a sleeping angel still.

When this misfortune happened, the kindly young fairy who had saved the princess by changing her sleep of death into this sleep of a hundred years, was twelve thousand leagues away in the kingdom of Mataquin. But being informed of everything, she arrived speedily in a chariot of fire drawn by dragons.

Then, being a fairy of great common sense and foresight, she suggested to the king and queen that she put them all to sleep for the next hundred years that they might all be together again when the young princess awoke. As soon as they agreed, and without asking anyone further, she touched each person and animal with her magic wand — the entire population of the palace — down to the horses that were in the stables and the grooms that attended them. With kind consideration for the feelings of the princess, she even touched the little fat lap-dog, Puffy, who had laid himself down beside his mistress on her splendid bed. He, like all the rest, fell fast asleep in a moment. The very spits that were before the kitchen-fire ceased turning, and the fire itself went out, and everything became as silent as if it were the middle of the night.

And soon the castle became hidden from all who wandered by, for in no time there sprung up around it a wood so thick and thorny that neither beasts nor men could attempt to penetrate there. Above this dense mass of forest could only be seen the top of the high tower where the lovely princess slept.

A great many changes happen in a hundred years. And so entirely was the story of the poor princess forgotten, that when a young prince from a neighboring kingdom, being one day out hunting and stopped in the chase by this formidable wood, inquired what wood it was and what were those towers which he saw appearing out of the midst of it, no one could answer him. At length, an old peasant was found who remembered having heard his grandfather say to his father that in this tower was a princess, beautiful as the day, who was doomed to sleep there for one hundred years until awakened by a king's son, her destined bridegroom.

At this, the young prince, who had the spirit of a hero, determined to find out the truth for himself. Spurred on by both generosity and curiosity, he leaped from his horse and began to force his way through the thick wood. To his amazement, the stiff branches all gave way, and the ugly thorns sheathed themselves of their own accord, and the brambles buried themselves in the earth to let him pass. This done, they closed behind him, allowing no one to follow. But, ardent and young, he went boldly on alone. The first thing he saw was enough to smite him with fear. Bodies of men and horses lay extended on the ground. But the men had faces, not death-white, but red as peonies, and beside them were glasses half filled with wine, showing that they had gone to sleep drinking. Next, he entered a large court, paved with marble, where stood rows of guards presenting arms, but motionless as if cut out of stone. Then he passed through many chambers where gentlemen and ladies, all in the costume of the past century, slept at their ease — some standing, some sitting. The pages were lurking in corners, the ladies of honor were stooping over their embroidery frames, or listening apparently with polite attention to the gentlemen of the court, but all were as silent as statues and as immoveable. Their clothes, strange to say, were fresh and new as ever, and not a particle of dust or spider-web had gathered over the furniture, though it had not known a broom for a hundred years.